EDGE
BOOKS™

The Real World of Pirates

PIRATE
HIDEOUTS

SECRET SPOTS AND SHELTERS

By Allison Lassieur

Consultant:
Sarah Knott, Director
Pirate Soul Museum
Key West, Florida

Capstone
press®

Mankato, Minnesota

Edge Books are published by Capstone Press,
151 Good Counsel Drive, P.O. Box 669, Mankato, Minnesota 56002.
www.capstonepress.com

Library of Congress Cataloging-in-Publication Data
Lassieur, Allison.
    Pirate hideouts: secret spots and shelters / by Allison Lassieur.
    p. cm.—(Edge Books. The real world of pirates)
    Summary: "Describes the places that pirates used as hideouts"—Provided
by publisher.
    Includes bibliographical references and index.
    ISBN-13: 978-0-7368-6426-8 (hardcover)
    ISBN-10: 0-7368-6426-1 (hardcover)
    1. Pirates—Juvenile literature. 2. Harbors—Caribbean Sea—Juvenile literature.
I. Title. II. Series.
G535.L296 2007
910.4'5—dc22   2006006999

Editorial Credits
Angie Kaelberer, editor; Thomas Emery, designer; Jason Knudson, illustrator; Kim
    Brown, production artist; Wanda Winch and Charlene Deyle, photo researchers

Photo Credits
Corbis/zefa/Sergio Pitamitz, 5
Ej.: *Plano de la Isla Tortuga, 1638*. España. Ministerio de Cultura. Archivo
    General de Indias, Secc. MP-VENEZUELA (24), 10
The Image Works/Mary Evans Picture Library, 18
Institute of Nautical Archaeology, 28
Mary Evans Picture Library, Douglas McCarthy, 9
(c) National Maritime Museum, London/Adam Willaerts, 16–17
North Wind Picture Archives, 24, 26
Peter Newark's American Pictures, 13, 14, 19, 20
Photo Researchers Inc./Lynette Cook, 22–23
Shutterstock/Lagui, 10; Ricardo Manuel Silva de Sousa, 7

1 2 3 4 5 6 11 10 09 08 07 06

TABLE OF CONTENTS

CHAPTERS

4 WHERE DID PIRATES HIDE?

11 PIRATES' PARADISE

16 WICKED CITY OF PORT ROYAL

24 WHAT HAPPENED TO THE HIDEOUTS?

FEATURES

30 GLOSSARY

31 READ MORE

31 INTERNET SITES

32 INDEX

Chapter One

WHERE DID PIRATES HIDE?

Pirate stories are full of legends about the places where pirates hid from the law. A few pirates are said to have hidden themselves and their treasures on deserted beaches. Legends also say that pirates hid in secret lagoons and on uncharted islands. Some pirates are believed to have lived in damp, dark caves.

Learn About:
- Hideout legends
- Golden Age of Piracy
- Pirate towns

Some pirates found safety
on deserted tropical islands.

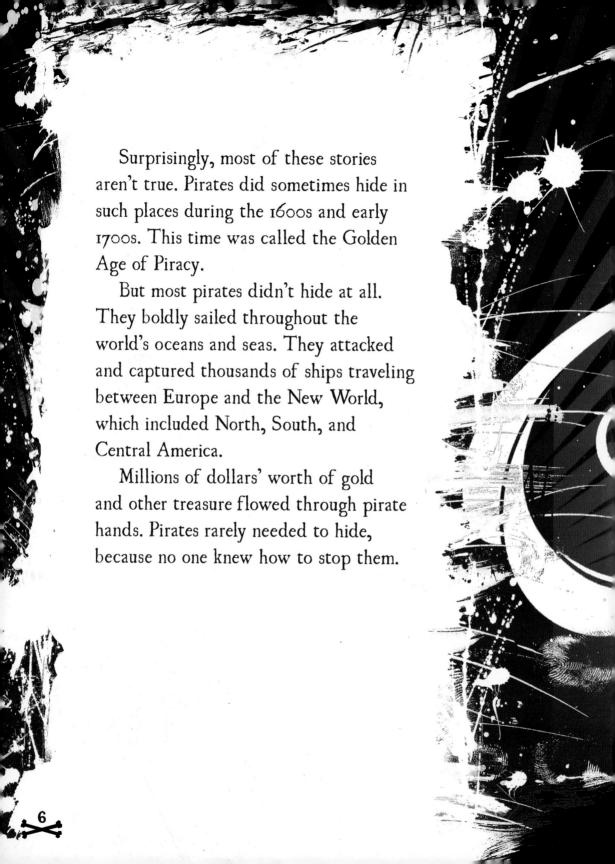

Surprisingly, most of these stories aren't true. Pirates did sometimes hide in such places during the 1600s and early 1700s. This time was called the Golden Age of Piracy.

But most pirates didn't hide at all. They boldly sailed throughout the world's oceans and seas. They attacked and captured thousands of ships traveling between Europe and the New World, which included North, South, and Central America.

Millions of dollars' worth of gold and other treasure flowed through pirate hands. Pirates rarely needed to hide, because no one knew how to stop them.

During the Golden Age of Piracy, pirate ships ruled the oceans.

Pirate Havens

Pirates did need safe places to rest, though. They needed harbors where they could careen and repair their ships. Pirates needed to buy food and other supplies. Most of all, they needed a place to spend their riches.

During the Golden Age of Piracy, several towns became pirate havens. They welcomed pirate ships and the treasures they brought. Merchants and farmers sold goods and food to pirate crews. Taverns did a brisk business whenever a pirate ship came to town. For more than 40 years, these towns thrived under the pirates' protection and good will.

EDGE FACT

Spain controlled much of the treasure that came out of the New World. The route from the coasts of South America through the Caribbean Sea was called the Spanish Main.

Townspeople often welcomed pirates and the business they brought.

The Spanish word *tortuga* means
"turtle." The island of Tortuga
near Hispaniola got its name
because it was shaped like a turtle.

Chapter Two

PIRATES' PARADISE

The Caribbean is known as one of the most beautiful areas in the world. Small islands dot the deep blue Caribbean Sea. The islands were close to the shipping routes between Central America, South America, and Europe. For pirates, these islands were the perfect paradise.

Hispaniola

The island of Hispaniola lies east of Cuba in the Caribbean Sea. Today, the countries of Haiti and the Dominican Republic make up the island.

In the early 1600s, the Spanish government controlled Hispaniola. The island was little more than a wilderness. Herds of wild cattle and pigs roamed the island.

Learn About:
- Caribbean pirates
- Buccaneers
- Tortuga

11

From Hunters to Pirates

Although Spain controlled Hispaniola, many Frenchmen were attracted to the good hunting opportunities on the island. These men were as wild and savage as the animals they hunted. They dressed in animal skins and lived off the land. The native Arawak people taught these hunters how to smoke meat on a wooden grill called a *boucan*. The French hunters were called *boucaniers*, or "buccaneers."

The buccaneers survived by trading animal meat and hides for supplies from passing ships. Sometimes, the buccaneers attacked the ships.

The Spanish government became alarmed at the number of buccaneers on Hispaniola. To get rid of them, the Spanish government sent hunters to kill all the animals. They thought that if the animals were gone, the buccaneers would leave. But the plan backfired. The starving buccaneers turned to piracy with a fury. They attacked almost every ship that sailed nearby.

Buccaneers used their wits and hunting skills to survive.

Turtle Island

Around 1630, buccaneers settled on a small, turtle-shaped island off Hispaniola's coast. Tortuga Island had fresh water, rich soil, and safe harbors.

Soon after, the French government took control of Tortuga. The governor promised safety to all ships—for a price. The governor also issued letters of marque to pirates. These letters allowed pirates to legally attack Spanish ships. In return, the pirates shared the treasure with the French government. Pirates flocked to the waters surrounding Tortuga in search of riches.

The Brethren of the Coast controlled much of the piracy in the Caribbean.

Brethren of the Coast

For 10 years, the buccaneers of Tortuga attacked Spanish treasure ships. They rarely left anyone on these ships alive.

Around 1640, the Tortuga buccaneers began calling themselves Brethren of the Coast. To be one of the Brethren, a pirate had to obey the pirate codes. These rules included deciding which ships to attack and how a treasure would be divided.

But the power of the Tortuga pirates didn't last. By the 1690s, the French and Spanish governments had made peace. Pirates were caught and hanged. No more money flowed into Tortuga. Businesses closed and people moved away. Once again, Tortuga was little more than a deserted island.

Chapter Three

WICKED CITY OF PORT ROYAL

British ships sailed to and from the ports of Jamaica.

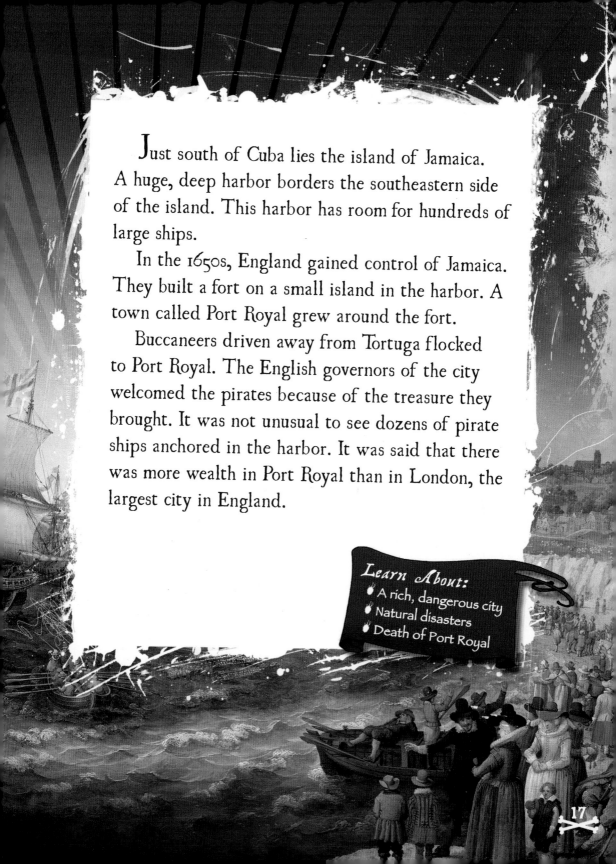

Just south of Cuba lies the island of Jamaica. A huge, deep harbor borders the southeastern side of the island. This harbor has room for hundreds of large ships.

In the 1650s, England gained control of Jamaica. They built a fort on a small island in the harbor. A town called Port Royal grew around the fort.

Buccaneers driven away from Tortuga flocked to Port Royal. The English governors of the city welcomed the pirates because of the treasure they brought. It was not unusual to see dozens of pirate ships anchored in the harbor. It was said that there was more wealth in Port Royal than in London, the largest city in England.

Learn About:
- A rich, dangerous city
- Natural disasters
- Death of Port Royal

Pirates came to towns to eat, drink, and have fun.

A Bustling Town

Soon, the small town was bursting with people who wanted to make money from the pirates. Merchants set up booths in the streets. They traded food, cloth, tools, and other items to the pirates. Taverns, hotels, and houses sprang up almost overnight.

Not surprisingly, Port Royal was a dangerous place. The pirates' wealth attracted thieves from all over the world. Townspeople were often robbed. Groups of raiders sometimes attacked the town. They stole gold and other treasure from shop owners. People fled from these raiders. But when the raiders left, the townspeople returned. They knew that another pirate ship and its treasures would soon come.

Port Royal's harbor was a safe place for pirate ships to dock.

EDGE FACT

With at least 7,000 people, Port Royal was one of the New World's largest cities.

Beginning in 1671, Port Royal's new governors captured and punished pirate captains and their crews.

When a pirate ship docked, a cheering crowd greeted it. People crowded around the ship to see what kinds of treasure would be unloaded.

Government officials claimed their share of the treasure first. The rest was sold to the highest bidder. The money was then divided among the pirates. Then, the people returned to town. They knew that soon the pirates would come to spend their loot on food, drink, warm beds, and other comforts.

The End of Port Royal

By the 1660s, Port Royal was one of the most famous cities in the world. But that soon changed. In 1671, new governors came to Port Royal. The new leaders passed laws against the pirates. They arrested and hanged many pirates.

It took more than the government to change life in Port Royal. On the morning of June 7, 1692, a huge earthquake struck Port Royal. Houses and buildings crumbled. A short time later, a tsunami engulfed the town.

The huge wave turned the beaches to quicksand. The quicksand sucked dozens of buildings underground. Every ship in the harbor was destroyed. At least 2,000 people died that day.

The survivors saved what things they could. Some left the island for good. Other people moved to the other side of the harbor. A few small villages were built. But none of these villages ever grew to the size and fame of Port Royal.

The earthquake that hit Port Royal triggered a huge tsunami that rolled over the town.

Chapter Four

WHAT HAPPENED TO THE HIDEOUTS?

By the early 1700s, the Golden Age of Piracy was ending. Most European countries were now at peace. They didn't need pirates to steal gold and treasure from enemy ships.

The Spanish had stolen vast amounts of gold from native people in the New World. But the gold ran out. There was little left for the pirates to steal.

Learn About:
- End of the Golden Age
- Hideouts today
- Searching for treasure

Piracy continued into the 1700s, but there was less treasure to go around.

With no treasure to steal, there wasn't a need for safe towns for pirates. The towns that had once been famous for their riches and wickedness were forgotten.

By 1750, pirates no longer ruled the world's seas and oceans.

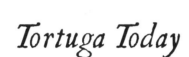

Tortuga Today

The turtle-shaped island of Tortuga is as beautiful today as it was in the days of the pirates. Long, white beaches stretch along the coast. But there are few people on the island. Fishermen camp on the island during certain times of the year. A few tourists enjoy the beaches and the ocean.

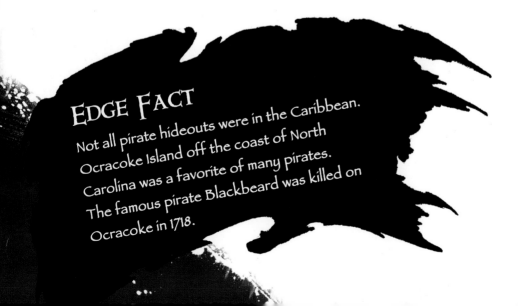

EDGE FACT

Not all pirate hideouts were in the Caribbean. Ocracoke Island off the coast of North Carolina was a favorite of many pirates. The famous pirate Blackbeard was killed on Ocracoke in 1718.

Lure of Old Port Royal

There is hardly anything left of the town of Port Royal. The natural disasters that destroyed it did their job well.

Today, a small, poor fishing village sits at the site of Port Royal. Tourists visit the area to see where the famous pirate town once stood.

Archaeologists come to Port Royal to dig up the ruins of the town. Scuba divers search the waters for artifacts. The objects they find help people learn about life in the 1600s and 1700s.

Some treasure hunters think that gold and jewels still lie somewhere in the harbor at Port Royal. They believe that the treasure sank with the ships when the earthquake hit. But no one has found pirate treasure at Port Royal—yet.

Today, scuba divers search the ocean floor
for remains of the treasures of Port Royal.

Glossary

archaeologist (ar-kee-OL-uh-jist)—a scientist who studies how people lived in the past

artifact (AR-tih-fakt)—an object made or used by people in the past

buccaneer (buhk-uh-NIHR)—a pirate in the Caribbean in the 1600s

careen (kuh-REEN)—to turn a ship on its side to clean or repair the hull

harbor (HAR-bur)—a place where ships load and unload passengers and cargo

haven (HAY-vuhn)—a place of rest and safety

tavern (TAV-urn)—a place where people can buy and drink alcoholic beverages

tsunami (tsoo-NAH-mee)—a very large wave caused by an underwater earthquake or volcano

Read More

Butterfield, Moira. *Pirates and Smugglers.* Kingfisher Knowledge. Boston: Kingfisher, 2005.

Platt, Richard. *Pirate.* DK Eyewitness. New York: DK, 2004.

Solway, Andrew. *A Pirate Adventure.* Fusion. Chicago: Raintree, 2006.

Internet Sites

FactHound offers a safe, fun way to find Internet sites related to this book. All of the sites on FactHound have been researched by our staff.

Here's how:

1. Visit *www.facthound.com*

2. Choose your grade level.

3. Type in this book ID **0736864261** for age-appropriate sites. You may also browse subjects by clicking on letters, or by clicking on pictures and words.

4. Click on the **Fetch It** button.

FactHound will fetch the best sites for you!

Index

Arawak people, 12
archaeologists, 28

Brethren of the Coast, 15
buccaneers, 12, 14, 15, 17

Caribbean Sea, 8, 11
caves, 4

earthquakes, 21, 23, 28
England, 17

France, 12, 14, 15

Golden Age of Piracy, 6, 8, 24

harbors, 8, 14, 17, 22, 28
Hispaniola, 11, 12, 14
hotels, 18

Jamaica, 17

letters of marque, 14

merchants, 8, 18

New World, 6, 8, 11, 19, 24

Ocracoke Island, 27

pirate codes, 15
pirate ships, 17, 18, 21, 22, 28
Port Royal, 17, 18, 19, 21, 22, 23, 28

raiders, 18

scuba divers, 28
Spain, 8, 11, 12, 14, 15, 24
Spanish Main, 8
supplies, 8, 12, 18

taverns, 8, 18
thieves, 18
Tortuga Island, 14, 15, 17, 27
trading, 12, 18
tsunamis, 21, 22, 23